THE ENCHANTED TUNNEL

BOOK ONE
PIONEER PUZZLE

THE ENCHANTED TUNNEL

BOOK ONE
PIONEER PUZZLE

Marianne Monson

Illustrated by Dan Burr

DESERET
BOOK

SALT LAKE CITY, UTAH

Library of Congress Cataloging-in-Publication Data
Monson, Marianne.
  Pioneer puzzle / Marianne Monson.
    p. cm. — (The enchanted tunnel series ; bk. 1)
  Audience: 4–6
  Summary: Twins Nathan and Aria discover that a tunnel under the stage in their church's cultural hall leads, magically, to another time when they find themselves on the pioneer trail with Joseph, a boy their age, and they must find their way back home.
  ISBN 978-1-60641-669-3 (paperbound)
  1. Time travel—Juvenile fiction. 2. Mormon pioneers—Juvenile fiction. 3. Pioneer children—Juvenile fiction. 4. Fantasy fiction, American. 5. Children's stories, American. [1. Time travel—Fiction. 2. Mormons—Fiction. 3. Frontier and pioneer life—Fiction. 4. Brothers and sisters—Fiction. 5. Twins—Fiction.] I. Title. II. Series: Monson, Marianne. Enchanted tunnel series ; bk. 1.
  PZ.M76282Pio 2010
  [Fic]—dc22   2010001320

Printed in the United States of America
Alexander's Print Advantage, Lindon, UT

10   9   8   7   6   5   4   3

For my grandmothers
Alice Allred and Nelda Monson
who have told me countless
pioneer stories

A BIG THANK-YOU

Special thanks to family members and friends who read the manuscripts in early stages and made suggestions, including Laura Byrd, Lexi King, Marilynn Monson, Nathan and Aria Burton, Brian King, and Becky Thornley Fargo. These books never would have happened without the talented faculty at Vermont College. Finally, I am grateful to Heidi Taylor at Deseret Book Company for her advice and enthusiasm about this project.

A NOTE TO THE READER

When I read a good book, I like to know if it *really* happened. *The Enchanted Tunnel* books are historical fiction, which means that part is true and part is made up. Nathan and Aria and their adventures in the enchanted tunnel are imagined, but the events from Church history are true. They *really* happened. We know about them from pioneer journals and other historical records.

Some of the details, such as what the characters were eating or doing on a specific day, are invented, but they are the types of things people of the time *often* ate or did. You can read more about the true stories that relate to Nathan and Aria's adventures by looking at the section called "To Learn More" on page 81 at the end of this book.

When I was a child, I sometimes found it difficult to relate to people from scripture stories because they lived so long ago. Thankfully, I had wonderful parents and teachers who brought the scriptures to life. These teachers opened a magic tunnel in my mind and helped me to imagine myself in the scripture stories. It is my hope that the *Enchanted Tunnel* books will do the same for you.

1

M&M'S OR CRICKETS?

"Nathan, would you put that away and sit up, please?" Brother King was Nathan's favorite Primary teacher, but he looked frustrated.

Nathan dropped the front legs of his chair back onto the floor. Then he returned his GPS system to his pocket.

"Do you remember what I was saying?" asked Brother King. He was holding a black-and-white picture of a pioneer boy. The boy wasn't smiling.

"I don't know," said Nathan. "Something about pioneers."

"I know!" said Aria.

"Of course you do," said Nathan. He

frowned. Sometimes it was annoying that his twin sister knew so much about history.

"You were saying that the pioneers didn't always have food to eat," said Aria. "Sometimes they had to eat prairie dogs."

"And even crickets," said Brother King.

Aria made a face.

Nathan's stomach grumbled. He was hungry. Maybe as hungry as a pioneer. He had eaten cereal for breakfast, but that seemed like a long time ago.

"Too bad pioneers didn't have peanut M&M's," said Nathan. Peanut M&M's were Aria's favorite candy.

Brother King laughed. "I wonder if a pioneer would like M&M's. Class, this week I want you to think about what it would be like to walk from here to Utah."

Brother King finished the lesson, and Nathan's friend Ben said the closing prayer.

"'Bye, Brother King," said Nathan. He left to find Mom.

"How was Primary?" she asked.

"Fine," said Nathan, "but I'm hungry. Can we go?"

"I have a quick meeting, and then we can go," said Mom.

"I'm starving!" said Nathan.

She dug through her bag. "Here are some crackers and a bag of M&M's. We'll have lunch soon." He knew it was no use to argue.

"Rats," he whispered.

Aria caught up to him.

"Mom has a meeting," said Nathan. "If Dad were here, he could take us home."

"But he's not," said Aria. "So let's play in the cultural hall. Are those M&M's?"

"Yeah, but if you want some, you'll have to catch me," said Nathan.

Nathan walked as fast as he dared in the hallway.

The twins burst into the cultural hall. Nathan hopped onto the stage and hid behind a cardboard pioneer wagon that had been left behind after a stake play. His sister followed him.

"Hand over those M&M's!" said Aria. She grabbed for them.

"No way!" said Nathan, laughing. He threw the M&M's into a box of costumes and sat on top of them.

Aria jumped on top of Nathan and tickled him in his most ticklish spot.

"Stop!" he squealed.

"Promise to move?" asked Aria. She was an expert tickler.

"Okay! Okay!" said Nathan. He jumped out of the box of costumes.

Aria put the candy to one side and started

digging through the box. "Wow!" she said. "Look at these! Pioneer hats and dresses. They look just like the ones in Brother King's book."

"I can't believe they used to wear those things," said Nathan.

"I would love to wear them!" said Aria.

Aria put a faded bonnet on her head and tied the bow. "This one looks really old," she said. "How do I look?"

"Like a pioneer girl who doesn't want M&M's!" said Nathan.

He snatched the M&M's and backed away.

"No fair!" said Aria. She held onto her bonnet and ran after him.

Nathan raced to the edge of the stage and looked around the large room. Where could he go?

Then he thought of the long storage

cupboard under the stage where the chairs were usually kept. The chairs were all set up, so the cupboard was empty.

Perfect.

2

INTO THE TUNNEL

Nathan stuffed the M&M's into his pocket and jumped off the stage. He flung open a door to the cupboard and crawled inside.

Yep, it was empty. Dark and cold, too.

He kept crawling. Soon the door was a little square of light behind him.

Would Aria follow?

"Get back here, Nathan Alex Hall!" said Aria.

Nathan looked back. His sister, still wearing that silly bonnet, was peering upside down through the open door.

"Come and get me!"

"Okay," said Aria. "You asked for it!"

She swung off the stage and started into the

cupboard. As soon as she entered, Nathan felt a shock run along the floor. It sizzled like electricity.

Weird! he thought. *What was that?*

He looked deeper into the cupboard, which now looked more like a tunnel than a storage area. He could see only blackness.

Where was the end?

"I'm going to tickle you till you can't stand up!" said Aria. She was getting closer.

"Aria," he said, "I think this tunnel goes on forever!"

Aria stopped and looked over her shoulder. "You're right. I can barely see the door now."

"Maybe we should go back," said Nathan.

"It must end somewhere," said Aria. "Give me my M&M's, and we can go back."

"No way!" said Nathan. He crawled forward and then stopped. The floor beneath him didn't feel like concrete any more. "Something really weird is going on!" he said.

"Do you feel like you're crawling over rocks?" asked Aria.

"Yes!"

"Me, too. Look—there's light ahead."

He lifted his head. She was right. There *was* light coming from an opening. And through the opening he could see scraggly bushes.

"Are we in a cave?" asked Nathan. "Where is the church? And Mom?"

"I don't know," said Aria, "but maybe someone out there does."

Nathan looked in the direction his sister was pointing. His mouth fell open. He could see a pioneer wagon, a *real* pioneer wagon, rumbling past.

3

WHERE ARE WE?

Nathan and Aria stood up.

"Come on," said Aria, twisting a strand of her light brown hair around her finger. She often did that when she was nervous. "Let's see where we are."

They moved closer to the opening. They seemed to be in a cave in the side of a mountain. Below them was a trail. Dozens of covered wagons were stopped nearby at the base of a hill.

Nathan could hear babies crying, animals snorting, and voices calling to one another. "It's so noisy!" said Nathan.

"And dusty," said Aria, coughing.

They made their way to the trail, where

tracks had been worn into the ground by wagon wheels.

"What's going on?" said Nathan. "Where are we?"

"Can't you guess?" said Aria.

"No," said Nathan.

"We must have found some sort of magic passageway back in time," said Aria. "We're on the pioneer trail!"

"*That* is what I was supposed to guess?" asked Nathan.

"It happens all the time in books," said Aria. "And kids in books are always surprised when they end up in another world. But I always thought something like that would happen to me."

"You *did?*" asked Nathan.

"At least I hoped it would."

"Well, I didn't," said Nathan. "And I want lunch."

From the direction of the pioneer camp, a cow mooed.

"It doesn't look like lunchtime here," said Aria.

She was right. The air was cold, and the sun was just rising. The leaves on the trees were beginning to turn gold and red.

"Maybe he has something you can eat," she said, pointing.

Nathan spun around. Behind them on the trail was a boy. A pioneer boy. He was walking toward them. And he was waving.

"Should we hide?" asked Nathan.

"Too late," said Aria.

4

A BOY WITH A BUCKET

"Hello!" said the boy.

He was wearing pants, a vest, a black hat, and boots. In one hand he carried a bucket of water.

"Hello," he said again.

Now that the boy was closer, Nathan could see that he was about his own age. His dark brown eyes looked worried.

"Have you seen an ox?" asked the boy.

Nathan and Aria shook their heads.

"We lost our oxen. Ma is afraid the other people won't wait."

Aria looked down the trail to the wagon camp. "Do you mean them?"

"Yes," said the boy. "Captain wants to leave right after breakfast."

"Breakfast?" said Nathan. That sounded good.

"Maybe we can help," said Aria.

Nathan looked at Aria. Had she lost her mind? What did they know about finding oxen?

The boy's face split into a grin. "Really? That would be swell! My brother, John, rode out to look for them too, but I'm sure he could use help. First I need to take Martha Ann this water for the dishes."

"Do you think there might be some extra breakfast?" asked Nathan.

Aria glared at him.

But the boy said, "Yep, there may be. My name is Joseph F."

"I'm Aria. This is Nathan."

"Are you with another wagon train?" asked Joseph F. He was looking at their clothes now.

"Well, sort of," said Aria.

Nathan realized how strange his white shirt and Sunday tie must look to the boy. *Good thing Aria put that silly hat on,* Nathan thought, wishing he had brought a hat himself.

Joseph F. stared at Aria's shiny black shoes. "I've never seen shoes like those before. Or a dress like that, either. Where do you come from?"

"Far away," said Aria. She tugged on her dress, trying to make it longer.

"Very far," agreed Nathan.

Joseph F. shrugged and started walking toward camp. "I think Martha Ann made johnny-cakes," he said.

Aria tugged on Nathan's sleeve and whispered into his ear. "We shouldn't eat their food, remember? Brother King said they hardly ever had enough."

"If they are having crickets, I don't want any," said Nathan.

"Shhh," said Aria.

"Crickets?" asked Joseph F., laughing. "Do you eat crickets?"

Nathan blushed. "No, I just heard that some pioneers do."

"We got supplies at Fort Bridger," said Joseph F. "Besides, I'd have to be half-starved before I'd eat a 'hopper!"

"Me too," said Nathan.

5

MILK COWS AND JOHNNYCAKE

They walked into camp. "Wow," said Aria. She felt as if she had walked right into a movie. Everyone was wearing dusty pioneer clothes. And everyone was busy. Kids were gathering sticks for firewood. Teens were washing dishes and packing things into wagons. Women were cooking over fires. Men were hitching up oxen.

No one seemed surprised to see them, although a few people stared at their clothes.

"I wish Brother King could see this!" said Nathan.

Aria nodded.

People called hello to Joseph F. as they passed. One man in a brown hat stopped him. "Any sign of those oxen?" he asked.

Joseph F. shook his head. "Not yet, but they'll turn up."

"I hope so," said the man. "Is John looking?"

Joseph F. nodded.

"Cap'n Lott was by a few moments ago asking about you," said the man. "He'll be ready to move out soon. I don't have to tell you he won't wait for your ma."

Joseph F. nodded and kept walking. He stopped at last in front of a wagon where a girl sat milking a cow. Aria looked at the big spotted cow and was impressed. The girl looked younger than Joseph F., maybe seven years old. She wore a blue dress and an apron. Two brown braids hung down her back. She had freckles on her cheeks.

She smiled up at Joseph F., who put down the bucket of water. He pulled playfully on one of her braids.

"Are you saving some cream for your favorite brother?" he asked.

"Perhaps, if you're nice," she replied.

"These are my new friends, Nathan and Aria," said Joseph F. "This is my sister, Martha Ann."

"Hello," said Martha Ann. She smiled and went back to milking the cow. Long, white streams squirted into the bucket.

"Where's Ma and the other kids?" asked Joseph F.

"Down by the stream washing up."

"Any breakfast left?" asked Joseph F.

"There's some johnnycake for you on the mess chest by the fire," said Martha Ann. "Will you clean the kettle with the wash water when you're done?"

"Sure, Sis," said Joseph F. He walked toward the fire, and Nathan followed him. He wasn't sure what johnnycake was, but it sounded better than crickets.

Aria stayed next to Martha Ann. "Aren't you afraid the cow might step on you?" she asked.

"Naw," said Martha Ann. "Lilly is sweet. Don't you milk?"

Aria shook her head. "I've never tried."

"Really?" Martha Ann looked shocked. "You can try if you like. Nothing to it. Just squeeze and pull." Martha Ann moved over, and Aria crouched beside her.

"Touch Lilly with your shoulder so she can feel where you are."

Aria leaned against the cow's side, which felt scratchy and smelled like grass. She reached out her hand and touched one of the cow's teats. It was warm and squishy. She pulled, but nothing came out.

"You have to squeeze harder," said Martha

Ann. "Don't worry. You won't hurt her. Put your hand higher."

Aria squeezed and pulled again. Milk squirted onto Martha Ann's dress.

"Good!" Martha Ann giggled. "Now aim for the bucket."

Aria tried again, and a thin stream squirted into the bucket. She squeezed and pulled for a few more minutes. Her shoulder hurt. "This is hard work," she said.

"I'll finish it," said Martha Ann. "Then we can make butter."

Martha Ann milked quickly until the bucket was full.

Aria noticed that her friend's hands were dry and red. *I bet she has to work hard,* thought Aria.

When the milking was finished, Martha Ann showed Aria how to skim the cream from yesterday's milk and pour the new milk into a crock. She put a little cream into a tin cup and poured the rest into a bucket.

Aria took the bucket. The wooden sides felt rough against her fingers. Martha Ann placed a lid on top. Then she took the bucket and hung it from a hook attached to the outside of the wagon box.

"Now what?" asked Aria.

"Once the wagon is going, the bumping will churn the cream into butter."

"Really?" said Aria. "Wow."

"As long as my brothers can find those pesky oxen, of course." Martha Ann smiled.

6

CAPTAIN LOTT

Martha Ann carried the tin cup to the campfire. Joseph F. was cleaning the kettle, and Nathan was chewing something that looked like a fluffy, yellow pancake.

He broke off a piece and handed it to Aria. "It's yummy," he said. "Want some?"

Aria took a bite. It was crumbly and warm but not sweet like cake at home.

"Delicious," said Aria.

"Here's some cream to wash it down," said Martha Ann.

Nathan tasted it and passed the cup to Aria. "It's like warm, thick milk," he said.

Aria sipped and handed the cup to Joseph F. "Mmmm," she said.

He gulped the rest down happily and licked his lips. "Thanks for saving it, Martha Ann. You know the cream is my favorite."

All around them, people were hitching up their oxen and packing things into wagons. Oxen grunted and stamped their hooves, kids called to each other, and pans rattled.

Martha Ann poured water onto the campfire. It hissed and smoked.

Just then a tall man rode up on a horse. He wore a hat and boots and had a dark, scraggly beard. His face was red, but Aria didn't think it was sunburned.

Nathan noticed that Martha Ann and Joseph F. did not look happy to see the man. Their faces reminded him of how he felt when his school principal walked into the classroom.

The man did not say hello. "Is that brother of yours back, Joseph F.?" he asked.

"No, Captain Lott. Not yet," said Joseph F.

Aria could tell from the look on his face that he did not like the captain.

The captain smiled, but it wasn't a nice smile. "We can't wait any longer for you. It's the last day of the journey. We want to get to the Salt Lake Valley by dark."

"You don't need to wait," said Joseph F.

"I always told your mother she would hold up the rest of us. Now you may have to spend a few nights on your own."

"My mother has never slowed you down," said Joseph F. His eyes burned. "We'll be fine."

The captain noticed Nathan and Aria. "You found more kids?" he asked. "That will make your travel even slower."

Joseph F. stood up straight and tall. "See you in the Valley, Captain," he said.

Nathan thought his new friend suddenly seemed much older. He was proud of Joseph F. for standing up to this man.

"Perhaps," said the captain. He turned his horse away.

"Move out!" he called to each wagon he passed. The wagons lined up and slowly moved onto the trail. Some of the pioneers waved to the children as they passed. They seemed sorry to leave them behind. A few minutes later, the children heard the creaking of wagons, the grunting of oxen, and the shuffling of walking feet.

"They're leaving you?" Nathan asked.

Martha Ann looked as if she was going to cry. "He's never liked Ma," she said. "He even said we poisoned his cattle. 'Course we didn't."

"Wish I could!" said Nathan. He was angry that the captain would be so mean.

Joseph F. shook his head. "Captain Lott wanted us to stay behind in Winter Quarters," he said. "He thought we would slow him down. Ma told him we would beat him to the

Salt Lake Valley, but I guess that's not likely now." Joseph F. shook his head.

Dust clouds billowed in the air behind the wagon train. The wagons slowly climbed up the hill.

Aria watched the wagons for a moment and then looked at Joseph F. and Nathan. "I think we should help find those oxen," she said. "If we find them soon, you won't be too far behind."

Joseph F. picked up his hat and put it on his head. "You're right, Aria. Will you be okay, Martha Ann?" he asked.

Martha Ann wiped her eyes. "You bet. Go find the oxen, Joseph F. I'll get Ma and the other kids. We'll be ready when you get back. Then we'll show Captain Lott we won't slow him down."

7

BERRY AND BROAD

"We need some rope," said Joseph F. He climbed into the wagon, and Nathan and Aria peeked inside the cover. Every corner of the wagon was filled with crates, barrels, and blankets. Pots and tools hung from hooks. Joseph F. lifted down two ropes.

"I think we should start with a prayer," he said, jumping out of the wagon.

"That's a good idea," said Nathan.

"Ma has prayed for the oxen lots of times on this trip," said Joseph F.

He took off his hat, and they folded their arms. Joseph F. said the prayer. The words he used were a little different from those in prayers Aria had heard before, but she felt warm and safe, just like at home.

Joseph F. led them away from the camp, and they walked along the trail. "Where do you think the oxen might have gone?" Aria asked.

Joseph F. shrugged. "I don't know, but John is on his horse. Let's try this way." He led them off the trail and into the bushes.

"It's dangerous to leave the trail," he said. "Sometimes people get lost. But there are three of us. We should be all right."

Aria gulped. She did not want to get lost in the mountains.

Aria and Nathan tried to keep up with Joseph F., but he was quick. Aria scraped her shiny black Sunday shoes on rocks and bushes. How was she ever going to explain this to her mother? *If* they ever got home again.

While they walked, Joseph F. told them

about his oxen. He seemed to think they were the best in the world.

"Berry is red and bony," Joseph explained. "Broad is spotted with long horns."

Horns? thought Nathan.

"But Thom is my favorite," said Joseph F. "He's one of my best friends. He's white, and I raised him from a calf. He's smarter than most men."

"How did he get lost if he's so smart?" Nathan asked.

"He's not lost," said Joseph F. "He and Joe are back at camp. It's the other two that are missing. See what I mean?" He winked.

Nathan and Aria followed Joseph F. deeper into the bushes.

"They might be looking for water," he said. "Let's look around the stream."

"Uh, okay," said Nathan.

"What would Brother King say about this?" whispered Aria.

"Joseph F. looks just like the boy in his book," said Nathan. "Except he's not black-and-white. And he's *real*."

"Of course he's not black-and-white, silly," said Aria.

"In the pictures everyone looks so serious," said Nathan. "But Joseph F. and Martha Ann are cool!"

"Berry! Broad!" Joseph F. called.

Nathan and Aria looked in the bushes around the stream.

"Berry!" called Aria. "Here, boy!"

"He's not a dog," said Nathan, laughing. He walked deeper into the bushes.

Suddenly, something shook the leaves of the bush right in front of him. "Whoa! What was *that?*"

A little chipmunk darted out and rushed up

the branch of a tree. It sat there chattering angrily.

Now Aria laughed. "I don't think that chipmunk could pull the wagon very far."

"Hmmm," said Nathan. "Probably not." He kept walking toward the stream.

Suddenly he stopped. He was looking right into the eyes of the biggest animal he had ever seen. It had a furry brown face and long pointed horns. It was chewing grass as it looked at Nathan with large brown eyes.

"Uh . . . ," said Nathan. "Joseph! I think I found him!"

"Are you sure it's not a squirrel?" said Aria, teasing.

"I'm sure," said Nathan.

"You really found him?" asked Joseph F.

He ran toward Nathan and saw the ox. "You found Broad! Do you want to rope him up?"

"That's okay," said Nathan, still staring at the horns.

"You can help," said Joseph F.

He made a loop with the rope and handed the other end to Nathan.

"Well . . . ," said Nathan.

He watched as Joseph F. threw the loop over one of Broad's horns.

Nathan's heart raced. Was he going to be stabbed? Broad was standing still. He didn't look as if he wanted to stab anyone.

Joseph F. pulled the loop of rope over Broad's other horn and took a quick step back. Then he pulled the rope tight.

"We got one," said Joseph F.

"Now what?" asked Nathan.

"Can you hold him while we look for Berry?"

Nathan swallowed. "Um, maybe," he said. He took the rope in his hands.

Broad picked up one foot and put it down

again. Nathan thought about how much it would hurt if that huge hoof stepped on him.

A few minutes later Aria called from a large clump of willows. "Make that two! I've found Berry!"

"Swell," said Joseph F.

He carried the rope to Aria and helped her tie him up.

Broad bent down to nibble some green grass. Nathan made sure his foot was far away from the ox's mouth.

Broad lifted his head back up and chewed thoughtfully.

Nathan looked at the huge animal and thought how tired Broad must be. He had pulled a wagon hundreds of miles across the plains and then through the mountains. No wonder he'd run away.

"You're almost there," said Nathan. "You

have one more mountain to go. I hope you get lots of water to drink in the Valley."

"Now that we have them," said Joseph F., "let's catch up with the captain!"

8

MOUNTAIN STORM

Suddenly Nathan realized that the sky overhead had turned dark and the air was cold. Angry black clouds raced across the sky.

He heard a shout behind him. "Nathan, quick!" Joseph F. called. "Tie Broad to a tree! Storm's coming!"

Nathan had heard of mountain storms before, but he had never realized how fast they could arrive. A few minutes later it didn't look like daytime anymore. Clouds the color of an awful bruise made it seem as if it were night. An icy breeze bent the trees and bushes in all directions.

"It shouldn't last long!" Joseph F. called over the wind. "Tie up Broad so he doesn't bolt!"

Nathan's hands shook. But he took the rope and looped it twice around a tree trunk. Then he held onto the end, pulling the rope as hard as he could.

Broad stamped and snorted. His eyes rolled in his head. Tossing his head, he tugged hard on the rope.

Nathan pulled back. "Please don't let the rope break," he prayed.

The wind howled around them, and rain began to fall. It was a cold, sharp rain that stung his hands and neck. His fingers quickly became wet and numb.

"Just hold onto the rope," he told himself. "Hold on!"

Broad turned his head, pulling on the rope.

The rope was cutting into Nathan's frozen hands, but he didn't let go. If Broad got lost in the storm, how would Joseph F. and his family ever get to the Valley?

"Please," Nathan prayed again, "don't let him get away."

Still holding tight, he moved closer to the ox. "It's okay," said Nathan. "You're all right."

Nathan's voice was shaking, but Broad seemed to calm down. The ox moved closer to Nathan. He was careful to stay away from Broad's horns.

Holding the rope in one hand, Nathan reached out with his other hand to touch the ox on his huge shoulder. He could feel Broad's strong muscles.

"It's okay," Nathan said again.

Broad turned his head and made a deep, sad sound. Nathan patted him.

The wind ripped leaves from the trees and blew them into Nathan's face. Raindrops stung his head and ran into his eyes. He tried to wipe them away. *So that's why they wear hats,* he thought miserably. Nathan thought of his dad and wished he were there to help.

Berry grunted and tossed his head. Nathan's hands were so numb he could barely feel them, but he knew he couldn't let go.

"Don't let the rope break!" Nathan repeated. His heart was beating like a drum. He couldn't hold on much longer.

Then, as quickly as they had come, the black clouds moved off across the sky. The wind calmed, and the rain slowed to a sprinkle. Sunshine began to fill the clearing.

"Wow!" said Nathan. The wet trees and bushes sparkled in the light.

"Are you okay?" Joseph F. called. "Did you hold him?"

Nathan stretched his fingers. His palms were scraped and his fingers felt frozen, but he had done it.

"Yeah!" he cried. "Yeah, I did!"

9

A HELPFUL COMPASS

Aria and Joseph F. led a bony, red ox into the clearing where Nathan and Broad were standing.

"It's a good thing you were here!" said Joseph F. "Mountain storms are fierce. I couldn't have held them both."

"What happens if they aren't tied up?" asked Aria.

"They can run off and get lost for days," said Joseph F.

"That would be awful," said Aria.

"Let's get back to the trail," said Joseph F.

The trees and bushes were no longer dusty. They looked freshly washed and sparkling clean. But the children's clothes were soaking wet and covered with twigs and leaves. Aria tried to brush off her dress, but that didn't make it look much better.

They headed back up the hill. The bushes looked the same in every direction.

"I thought the trail was right here," said Joseph F. "Could have sworn it."

"Maybe it's that way," said Aria, pointing.

They walked to where she pointed, but there were just more willows and bushes. The hills went on and on.

"Ma is going to be worried," said Joseph F.

So is our ma, thought Aria.

"I'm hungry," said Nathan. Then he remembered the snacks in his pocket. "I have graham crackers and M&M's," he said.

"Graham crackers?" asked Joseph F.

"Try one," said Nathan. He handed a cracker to him and another to Aria.

Aria chewed gratefully. Nathan ate his in one bite.

Joseph F. looked at the cracker. "How do you make these?" he asked.

Aria tried not to laugh. "We didn't make them," she replied. Then she asked her brother, "Do I still have to tickle you for the M&M's?"

Nathan handed them over. Aria gave Joseph F. a red M&M. "Try this. It's my favorite."

He popped it in his mouth. "Wow!" he said. "A sweet. With a nut inside."

"Better than crickets?" asked Aria. She handed him some more.

"Much better than crickets!" said Joseph F.

Nathan's hand bumped against the GPS system in his pocket. He pulled it out.

"That's not going to work here," said Aria.

Nathan nodded but looked at the screen just in case. "Hey." He pushed a button. "It *is* working!" He pushed again. "It says we're on Little Mountain in Utah."

"This mountain doesn't look so little to me," said Aria.

"What kind of compass is that?" asked Joseph F.

"A really helpful one," said Aria.

Nathan looked at the GPS. "The trail should be up there," he said, pointing up the hill.

"Let's go, Berry and Broad," said Joseph F. "You have to pull the wagon one last time."

10

PIONEER CHILDREN

Nathan tugged on Broad's rope. The ox looked stubborn for a moment but stopped chewing and followed Nathan.

Near the top of the hill, they found the trail. "Here it is!" said Nathan.

"And there is John!" said Joseph F. They looked down the trail and saw a teenage boy on horseback riding in their direction. He was waving his hat and shouting. When he caught up to them, he said, "You found them! Great work, little brother!"

"Maybe if we hurry we can still make it to the Valley before dark," said Joseph F.

John reached down to slap Joseph F. on the back. "Why don't you run ahead and tell Ma so she can stop worrying? I'll take care of Berry and Broad."

"Okay, come on," said Joseph F. He handed John the ropes and set off running. Nathan and Aria raced to keep up. They followed the trail back to camp. Only one covered wagon remained.

A woman in a yellow bonnet and dress came around the side of the wagon. She was looking up and down the trail in both directions.

"Joseph F.?" she called when she saw him. "Is it you?"

"Yes, ma'am," called Joseph F. "I found 'em!"

The woman ran forward and hugged Joseph F.

"Well done! When the storm came, I was worried they would be lost for good!"

"They would have if I hadn't had help," said Joseph F. "Nathan and Aria helped me hold 'em."

"Thank you for helping," said the woman. "I was praying for Joseph F., and you were just what he needed. I'm Sister Smith. Widow Smith, they call me."

Joseph F.'s mother had an English accent that made her sound like a proper lady. Her dark hair was pulled into a bun underneath her bonnet. Her brown eyes were beautiful, but she looked very tired.

Suddenly Aria made a strange choking sound.

"Are you all right?" asked Nathan. She nodded. "I'll tell you later," she whispered.

Sister Smith smiled. "Here is John with the oxen! Now, let's hitch up this wagon and see if we can keep up with the company."

"Do you think we can?" asked Joseph F.

Sister Smith nodded. "The storm may have scattered their cattle, too. It could be that we will beat them to the Valley after all."

Sister Smith gathered three other children while Joseph F. and John hitched Berry and Broad to the wagon.

Martha Ann gave Joseph F. a hug. "I knew you would find them!"

She turned to Nathan and Aria. "Were you scared during the storm?"

Nathan and Aria looked at each other. "Uh-huh," they both said at once. Then they laughed.

"The Lord answered our prayers," said Sister Smith. "We should give thanks." Joseph F. and John pulled off their hats. They folded their arms. Sister Smith prayed. Aria could tell she meant every word.

When the prayer ended, Aria looked at Sister Smith. She thought about her taking all these children across the plains and telling Captain Lott she would beat him to the valley. Aria knew this woman must be very brave.

"Giddyup!" said John. The oxen slowly started forward. Sister Smith walked beside the oxen, guiding them along the trail.

Nathan and Aria walked behind the wagon with the other children. Aria hummed a Primary song, "Pioneer Children Sang As They Walked." She looked at her shoes. They were scraped and dusty. And she had been a pioneer for only a few hours!

Soon they reached the top of the hill and looked down to the valley far below. Sister Smith stopped the wagon.

"Look at the view!" said Aria.

Mountains stretched as far as they could see. Below them, the valley was filled with a soft, purple mist. In the distance, they could see a spot of shiny silver.

"It's the Great Salt Lake," said Joseph F.

Aria noticed tears in Sister Smith's eyes. "A

temple will be built in this valley someday," she said. "And we won't ever have to leave it."

Aria looked at the empty valley and remembered the beautiful Salt Lake Temple she had seen when their family had visited Utah. "No, you won't," she said.

Sister Smith suddenly seemed to remember Nathan and Aria. She turned. "Where is your family?" she asked. "I don't want them to worry."

"They aren't far away," said Aria, hoping her words were true. "We'd better go now."

"Yeah," said Nathan.

"Thank you very much," said Sister Smith.

"I don't have any fancy sweets," said Joseph F., "but here are some Indian beads."

He put three blue beads into Aria's hand.

"Thank you," said Aria. "Where did you get them?"

"I found 'em on an anthill. The ants collect them."

"Neat." Aria put the beads in her pocket. "Thank you."

Martha Ann gave Aria a hug. "You'll have to do the milking at home now that you know how."

Aria smiled. "I'll need to ask my mother about that."

Nathan and Aria watched the wagon move slowly down the hill, the children walking behind.

Joseph F. and Martha Ann waved until they were out of sight.

11

BACK IN TIME

"I'm glad they are okay," said Nathan, "but how do we get home?"

"Do you think the tunnel will take us back again?" asked Aria.

"I hope so!"

They walked back down the hill and searched for the opening in the rock.

"Here it is!" said Aria.

"Nice work," said Nathan. They stared inside. It was so dark they couldn't see anything.

"I wish we had a flashlight," said Aria.

"Well, I didn't think we were going to end up on a pioneer trail today, or I'd have brought one," said Nathan.

Aria giggled.

They ducked into the cave and waited for their eyes to adjust to the dark.

Nathan moved to the back of the cave where a low tunnel began. He knelt down and started to crawl. "My hands are sore from holding Broad's rope."

"Mine are sore from milking," said Aria. She knelt down, too. A sizzle of electricity passed through the ground.

"Did you feel that?" asked Aria.

"Yeah," said Nathan.

The tunnel was completely black.

"I can't see a thing!" said Aria.

They crawled over rocks and stones. After a few minutes, the ground felt smooth under their hands.

"There's light ahead," said Nathan. It was a square of light. The cupboard door!

"We made it!" said Nathan. "We're at the church."

They pushed through the door and stood up. They were in the cultural hall.

Nathan and Aria looked at their clothes. Aria's shoes were ruined. Nathan's pants were torn and dusty.

"Mom is going to kill us," said Aria.

Nathan remembered something. "What were you going to tell me later?"

"I think I know who those people are," said Aria. "But I need to get home to find out for sure."

The door to the cultural hall opened, and their mother appeared.

"I'm finished with my meeting," she said. "We can go home now."

She looked at them in amazement. "What happened to your church clothes?"

Nathan and Aria looked at each other.

"We're really sorry!" said Aria.

"We didn't mean to," said Nathan.

"How could you possibly do that to your clothes in *here?*" she asked.

"That," said Nathan, "is a long story."

12

HE WAS WHO?

Aria was happy. She was clean after a warm bath, and her tummy was full from a delicious Sunday dinner. She couldn't help thinking about Joseph F. Had he made it to the Valley? She was pretty sure that even if he had, he wouldn't have found a warm dinner and bath waiting for him.

She knocked on Nathan's bedroom door. "Are you coming?" she asked.

"Yeah," said Nathan. They went into the kitchen, where the family's computer was kept.

"Mom, could we look up something about pioneers on the computer?"

"Sure," Mom replied. She opened an Internet

window for them and went back to what she was doing.

"Who do you think he was?" asked Nathan.

Aria typed in "Joseph F. Smith." An article came up.

"Joseph F. Smith was born on November 13, 1838," she read. "His father, Hyrum Smith, was killed in Carthage Jail with his uncle the Prophet Joseph Smith. When Joseph F. Smith was ten years old, he helped his mother, Mary Fielding Smith, travel to Utah and settle in the Salt Lake Valley. He became President of the Church on October 17, 1901."

"No way!" Nathan said excitedly. "That boy with the ox . . . became a prophet?"

"*And* he was Joseph Smith's nephew," said Aria.

"Wow," said Nathan. "That means . . . we helped a prophet find his ox."

"He wasn't a prophet yet," said Aria. "But

look at this." She read: "The last day of the journey, a sudden mountain storm scattered the cattle in the pioneer company. They spent hours finding the cattle. Mary Fielding Smith was the first in their group to arrive in the Salt Lake Valley."

"They made it!" said Nathan. He looked thoughtful. "Joseph F.'s father died when he was really young."

"We have a lot in common, even though he lived a long time ago," said Aria.

"It's a good thing we found that tunnel," said Nathan.

Aria nodded. "I think maybe we were supposed to find it."

"Do you think it will work again?"

"I'm not sure," said Aria. "I hope so. But if we go back, we'd better wear different clothes!"

"And take a flashlight," Nathan added.

Aria pulled the Indian beads out of her

pocket and held them in her hands. "These are beads Joseph F. Smith found on the pioneer trail," she said.

"No one would ever believe it," said Nathan. He laughed.

"What?" asked Aria.

"On Sunday, I'm going to tell Brother King that pioneer kids *do* like M&M's."

Aria smiled.

EPILOGUE

Joseph F. Smith left Nauvoo with his family a few months before his eighth birthday. His half-brother, John, had gone ahead with another company, so Joseph F. drove one of the family's wagons to Winter Quarters. After spending two years in Winter Quarters, the Smith family was ready to go west.

Mary Fielding Smith had seven children to take across the plains. Cornelius Lott, a captain in Heber C. Kimball's pioneer company, felt they weren't prepared for the journey. He told her, "If you start out in this manner, you will be a burden on the company the whole way, and I will have to carry you along or leave you on the way."

But Mary wanted to take her family to Zion. She replied, "I will beat you to the Valley and will ask no help from you either."

Along the way, the family encountered many challenges. Once one of their oxen fell down in exhaustion, and the captain thought it was dead. He said, "I told you you would have to be helped."

But Mary produced a bottle of consecrated oil and asked her brother and another elder to anoint and bless the ox. The ox got up and continued pulling as if nothing had ever happened.

Another time, the oxen became lost. Joseph and his uncle Joseph Fielding searched for hours but couldn't find them. Joseph F. returned to his mother and found her praying. She arose from her knees with a smile on her face.

A man told her he had seen her cattle and

pointed in one direction. Mary walked in the opposite direction, right to the spot where the man had tied the oxen in a clump of willows so he could steal them later.

On the last day of their journey west, the company stopped for the night at the base of Little Mountain in Emigration Canyon. They planned to enter the Salt Lake Valley the next day. But when the family awoke, their oxen were missing. John left on horseback to find them. The captain told the rest of the company to move on without the Smith family.

After a time, the Smiths' oxen were found. Then a sudden mountain storm frightened the company's cattle. The captain ordered the people to turn the panicked oxen loose in order to save the wagons from being overturned. A short time later, the storm subsided, and the Smiths continued their journey.

The family passed the other wagons, whose

owners were searching for their own now-scattered oxen. Mary's brother asked her if they should wait. She replied, "Joseph, they have not waited for us, and I see no necessity for us to wait for them."

The Smith family arrived at the Old Fort in the Salt Lake Valley that same night, September 23, 1848. The next morning was Sunday, and they listened to President Brigham Young speak. The other wagons arrived that afternoon.

The Smiths did indeed get to the Valley before the rest of their company, arriving twenty hours ahead of Captain Lott. Not long afterwards Mary Fielding Smith wrote, "Blessed be the God and Rock of my salvation, here I am, and am perfectly satisfied and happy, having not the smallest desire to go one step backward" (*Life of Joseph F. Smith,* 145).

Mary Fielding Smith's faith in the Lord's

protection and her reliance on prayer became an inspiration to Joseph F., who often spoke of her example throughout his life. He was only thirteen when she died in 1852. He once said of her, "Nothing beneath the Celestial Kingdom can surpass my deathless love for the sweet, noble soul who gave me birth—my own, own, mother" (*Life of Joseph F. Smith,* 4).

FUN FACTS

Joseph F. really did love milk. When he was a young child, his uncle the Prophet Joseph Smith told him he was pale from drinking so much milk.

Joseph F.'s favorite ox was named Thom. He said Thom was one of his most faithful friends. When things were difficult on the trail, he sometimes put his arms around Thom's neck and cried.

Many pioneers made necklaces and other jewelry from the Indian beads they found on the trail. Ants collected them, so they were often found around ant hills.

Joseph F. adored his little sister, Martha Ann. After they arrived in the Salt Lake Valley, they attended school together. One day, some time after their mother, Mary Fielding Smith, had died, a teacher threatened unfairly to punish Martha. Joseph F. told the teacher he could not whip his sister. When the teacher insisted, Joseph F. punched the teacher. He was expelled from school, and President Brigham Young called him on a mission to the Sandwich Isles (now Hawaii) even though he was only fifteen years old.

As a prophet, Joseph F. Smith was known for being loyal and courageous. He was a bold teacher and defender of the truth. His vision of the dead is now recorded in Doctrine and Covenants 138. During his final illness, he disobeyed his doctor's orders so that he could speak at general conference one last time.

TO LEARN MORE

You can learn more about Joseph F. Smith by reading in these books yourself or by asking a parent or teacher to help you:

Boys Who Became Prophets, by Lynda Cory Robison (Salt Lake City: Deseret Book, 2000).

Life of Joseph F. Smith: Sixth President of The Church of Jesus Christ of Latter-day Saints, compiled by Joseph Fielding Smith (Salt Lake City: Deseret Book, 1938).

RECIPE FOR JOHNNYCAKE

Johnnycakes are like fluffy pancakes. The pioneers folded the johnnycakes and put them in their pockets to stay warm until they were ready to eat them. You can bake these johnnycakes in an oven or cook them in a frying pan, as Martha Ann would have done.

1¼ cups flour
¾ cup cornmeal
½ tsp. salt
2 tsp. baking powder
1 egg, beaten
1 cup milk
¼ cup melted butter

In a medium-sized bowl, mix together the flour, cornmeal, salt, and baking powder.

In another bowl, combine the egg, milk, and melted butter.

Mix the dry and wet ingredients together and stir just until combined.

Pour batter into a greased 9x13-inch pan and bake for 30 minutes in an oven preheated to 400 degrees Fahrenheit.

Or pour about ¼ cup batter for each johnnycake into a greased frying pan heated to medium-high on the stove top. Turn over the johnnycake when it looks bubbly.

ABOUT THE AUTHOR

Marianne Monson spent much of her childhood looking for magic passageways. Reading good books has always been one of her favorite adventures. She studied English at Brigham Young University and also spent a semester in Jerusalem, where she crawled through Hezekiah's Tunnel. Now she particularly enjoys following her children, Nathan and Aria, as they discover their own enchanted tunnels.

Marianne holds an MFA from Vermont College in writing for children and young adults. She teaches creative writing at Portland Community College and serves as a Gospel Doctrine teacher in her ward in Hillsboro, Oregon. You can visit her at www.MarianneMonson.com.